Now You See Me

Now You See Me

HONEY POT COLLECTION

Ali Whippe

4 Horsemen
Publications, Inc.

4 Horsemen Publications, Inc.
1497 Main St. Suite 169
Dunedin, FL 34698
4horsemenpublications.com
info@4horsemenpublications.com

Cover by Battle Goddess Productions
Editor Nita Edetor

Ebook ISBN: 978-1-64450-239-6
Print ISBN: 978-1-64450-238-9
Audio ISBN: 978-1-64450-271-6

Dedication

For all the boys who like to watch

Chapter One

12:01 pm [Dylan: Wake up, Sorina.]

12:03 pm [Sorina: Yes, Master. I am awake, sir. May I use the bathroom?]

12:04 pm [Dylan: You may. Finish your morning routine in eleven minutes. Text me when you are in the kitchen.]

12:04 pm [Sorina: Yes, Master.]

12:14pm [Sorina: I am in the kitchen, Master.]

12:14 pm [Dylan: You are early, Sorina. I may have to punish you later.]

12:15 pm [Sorina: As you wish, Master.]

12:16 pm [Dylan: You may have your coffee now, but no sugar today. Eat a strawberry yogurt.]

12:16 pm [Sorina: Thank you, Master. I will be more precise tomorrow.]

12:17 pm [Dylan: Yes, you will. I need you ready for tonight, though. Are you wearing the bra and panties I picked out?]

12:17 pm [Sorina: Of course, Master.]

12:20 pm [Dylan: Good girl. Send me pictures. Close-up of you wearing the bra first. Panties next. Then your entire midsection in one picture without knees or face.]

12:22 pm [Sorina: Download Attached Image.]

12:24 pm [Sorina: Download Attached Image.]

12:25 pm [Sorina: Download Attached image.]

12:30 pm [Dylan: Very nice, Sorina. You have done well. Now lay the dress you will wear tonight on the bed and send me a picture. Then a picture of your feet in the shoes I chose.]

12:33 pm [Sorina: Download Attached Image.]

12:34 pm [Sorina: Download Attached Image.]

12:37 pm [Dylan: Excellent. I will be there to pick you up at 10:00 tonight. I expect you to be ready.]

12:38 pm [Sorina: Yes, Master.]

12:39 pm [Sorina: Master, is there anything else I should do to prepare for tonight?]

12:40 pm [Dylan: Not yet. Get to work, Sorina. You have ten minutes before you need to leave. Remember the list.]

*S*orina puts her phone down on the kitchen table and finishes the last sip of her coffee, putting the mug in the sink and tossing the empty yogurt container. Throwing on a pair of jeans and her Empire Records t-shirt, she checks herself in the mirror one more time before heading out for the day. Her simple makeup is enough to subtly flatter her normal good looks, highlighting her eyes and showcasing her pouty lips. She's glad she got the morning routine down to ten minutes— Dylan had been so disappointed when she still took over twenty minutes to get up. Now every motion is planned, each moment accounted for, and the general feeling of chaos doesn't take hold in her gut so easily. He'd been right, of course; simple routines help her so much. Him telling her what to wear helps more. His orders are always simple, direct, and within her ability—another thing that calms her raging nerves.

Her life is chaotic enough without having to make all those little decisions. Not that it's complicated—she works at a record store, finding vinyl albums for diehard fans who wander in but mostly packing up the orders that flow in online. She listens to music all day long, a perk, but sometimes the customers who do stroll in can be condescending. They see her long blonde hair and huge tits and assume she's just a pretty face. She doesn't bother telling them that she has their inventory memorized, that she can tell them where each album is in the store, nor does she mention that she plays six instruments and reads sheet music or that she can recite the history of most of the bands they carry—each album and track list burned into her brain.

Of course, all that knowledge makes it hard to recall other things, like the password for her bank account or where she put her keys.

Dylan has helped with all that, establishing tiny routines and checking on her to make sure she follows through, punishing her when she fails.

Sorina likes the punishments a little too much sometimes, and occasionally she deliberately flouts an order just to see what will happen.

She obeys another of his commands before leaving, checking off each item on her mental list as he instructs: dinner—yes, phone—yes, purse—yes, keys—yes, everything turned off in the apartment—yes, lock the door—yes. She heads down the stairs, a bounce in her step as she walks the block to the store.

"Hey!" Jenelle says as Sorina walks through the glass door. The middle-aged owner of the record store sits at the long counter, a mostly eaten sandwich still open on the paper in front of her. "On time again!" Jenelle smiles, tucking dark hair behind her ear and pushing up her glasses as she looks Sorina over. "I don't know what you're doing, girl, but keep it up. It's working!"

Sorina smiles at her boss, thinking of Dylan's control in her life, and walks behind the counter to join her. She tucks the Tupperware containing her dinner in the small fridge behind the counter, checks to make sure the store keys are in her purse, then sets it in the drawer below the register. "I'm trying a new thing," Sorina says vaguely. "I like it."

"So do I!" Jenelle says, taking a final bite and crumbling the rest of the paper, tidying her lunch as she gets to her feet, abandoning the single stool behind the counter. She tosses everything in the trash can, then finishes the rest of her bottled water. Sorina has casually mentioned that Jenelle should just bring a bottle and keep refilling it, but her boss doesn't seem interested in conserving plastic. She's more into conserving vinyl albums. Sorina puts her large water bottle on the counter, a subtle gesture that is lost on her boss.

"I did all the orders from yesterday and this morning," Jenelle says, nodding at the clipboard next to the register—another wasteful habit of printing everything on paper—but Jenelle insists on her system. Sorina looks over at the table against the wall beyond the counter. A pile of packages rests there, waiting for the mail carrier to pick them up. A decent day, and it's early yet.

"Nice," Sorina says, settling onto the stool Jenelle abandoned. "Thanks." She looks around the small store, the racks of albums, the posters lining the available wall space. "Anything I should work on today?"

Jenelle shrugs. "Nah. You did a great job re-sorting the punk section last time. Take it easy today. Just pack up anything that comes through online."

"Will do," Sorina agrees. She enjoys organizing, the practice soothing her mind, even if it sometimes means crawling around on

7

her hands and knees in the back corners, but she wants to save her energy for tonight. "See you Sunday then?"

Jenelle nods. "You have anything exciting planned for your day off tomorrow?"

Sorina shakes his head, "Nah. Just going to get some things done. The usual." She imagines Jenelle's expression if she told her boss what she would be doing after work tonight.

The cage. I hope it's the cage. He said I could if I was good. I've been so, so good.

"Really?" Jenelle asks, a small frown on her lips. "You should go out, have a good time, a young girl like you. You should have some fun in this city, have a night on the town!"

Sorina laughs, wondering what Jenelle's idea of a night on the town is. Her own involves leather cuffs and blindfolds, strangers and that electric excitement of being at their mercy. "Maybe," she says.

Jenelle rolls her eyes. "You're only young once, you know. Trust me. I should have had more fun when I was your age."

"Then I'll try to have enough fun for both of us," Sorina offers. "Maybe I'll go to the park or something."

Jenelle shakes her head, retrieving her purse from beneath the counter and logging out of the computer. "I'll see you Sunday," she says as Sorina logs in, officially taking over the store for the day. After her boss leaves, Sylvia pulls out the paperback stashed in her bag and rests it on the counter.

It's a classic kind of day, so she heads into the store to find something traditional to match.

Chapter Two

*S*orina is taking a break from her book to stretch her legs, walking the store and straightening the few out of place items, her need for perfect organization kicking in hard, when her phone chimes. The chime is a message from Dylan, and she scurries back to the counter to check it. Other messages can be ignored, like calls from her mother or texts from her few friends, but Dylan must be answered immediately.

5:45 pm [Dylan: Are you alone?]
5:45 pm [Sorina: Yes, Master.]
5:46 pm [Dylan: Go where no one on the street can see you.]

Sorina looks around the small store, settling on the empty space in the back behind the center aisle of records. It's her her best chance of semi-privacy without going into the bathroom. But Dylan hadn't said the bathroom. He'd just said to avoid the street. She stands in the small area at the back of the store, scanning the two glass windows that overlook the street. They are covered with posters and advertisements, but the glass still has a few clear spaces where someone could peer inside. The bottom of the door is definitely clear, but the top is covered by their store hours and a few announcements. She's fairly sure that anyone looking in would only see her head anyway, the rest hidden by the shelving.

5:47 pm [Sorina: I'm here. They can see my head if they look inside but nothing else.]
5:47 pm [Dylan: Good girl. Now put your hand up your shirt and squeeze your nipple through your bra.]

Low heat pools in Sorina's belly, and she rests the phone on the edge of the display, hand slowly skidding up the sensitive skin of her stomach, over the pink lace bra he chose for her, and she squeezes her nipple softly.

5:48pm [Dylan: Lift up your shirt. Pull your breast free from the bra. Lick your nipple, then blow on it.]

Sorina grins, looking around the store even though she knows there aren't any cameras in here. Jenelle wouldn't know how to work them even if she did own them. She lifts her shirt slowly anyway, rolling it above her breasts, then lifts one out as instructed, the weight heavy in her hand as she bends down to lick her nipples. She can't actually suck her nipple, which is what she wants to do, but she can lick the general area. Her double Ds make it easy to reach. She waits a moment, then blows, the cool air on her wet skin causing her to tremble, the hair on her arms standing on end.

"Mmm," she moans, a shiver racing through her. She drops her breast and reaches for the phone.

5:50 pm [Sorina: Yes, Master. Thank you, Master. What next, sir?]
5:50 pm [Dylan: Slide your fingers into your pants and feel yourself. Don't unbutton them. Tell me how wet you are.]

Sorina obeys, eager finger sliding between her waistband and her skin, dipping beneath the line of her matching pink panties to slide over her newly smooth skin. Another of Dylan's orders—get waxed for tonight. She smiles, the zing of pleasure shooting through her at the touch, and she removes her finger, the tip glistening with moisture. She reaches for the phone again.

5:51 pm [Sorina: Juicy, sir.]
5:51 pm [Dylan: Taste yourself. Tell me how you taste.]

Sorina slides her finger between her lips, savoring the taste on her tongue, wondering when Dylan will let her lick a pussy again. She loves cock, his cock—any cock, really—but pussy is still fascinating, all smooth and silky—the few she's licked anyway. Her nipples harden at the memory.

5:53 pm [Sorina: Like honey, sir. Sweet and musky.]
5:54 pm [Dylan: Unbutton your pants. Push them down your legs to your ankles. Leave the panties on but push them aside. Finger yourself. Hard. Fast. I expect you to come when I send my next message.]

Sorina puts the phone back down, resting it on top of the records in front of her, unbuttons her pants, and glances quickly at the street. She can see a few shapes on the sidewalk outside, but no one slows or touches the door. She yanks her pants down, feeling the cool air of the store on her bare legs, and that low pull in her belly twinges, pleasure spiraling out from her core at the idea of being so exposed at work.

Anyone can see me right now. Anyone at all.

Her hand drifts down to her panties, moving them aside as instructed, and she slides a finger inside, forgoing the pleasure of her clit to obey her master. It feels good, and she recalls his instructions: Hard. Fast. A second finger joins the first, then she uses her other hand to press hard against her clit as she moves her hand furiously. She squeezes tight around herself, the friction maddening. It's nice, but she knows that even if she comes, she will still want more, still want a cock to fill that space. Coming on fingers is good, but never great. Still, the thought of being naked and masturbating in the open like this at work is enough to add an edge, and her body tightens. She is dangerously close to the edge, but she knows she must wait for permission.

Wait, she commands herself. *Wait....wait for...*

It's too much. The naughtiness. The public display. All of it. She comes hard, shuddering on her fingers. An instant later, her phone buzzes.

5:58 pm [Dylan: Come for me, Sorina. Come now.]

Already there, sir.

She stands there for a moment before responding, the tiny act of rebellion making her smirk.

5:59 pm [Sorina: Thank you, sir.]
5:59 pm [Dylan: That was fast, Sorina. Very fast.]

Sorina bites her lip, guilt surging through her on the heels of her pleasure.

6:00 pm [Dylan: Did you wait for me, Sorina? Were you a good girl?]

Standing with her pants around her ankles and her shirt tucked above her boobs, Sorina stares down at her phone, a wave of heat flooding her, and not from the orgasm.

I can lie. He won't know. But I will know. Besides, he may punish me...

The prospect is enough to make her decide for truthfulness.

6:01 pm [Sorina: I am sorry, Master. I tried.]

Three long minutes pass, and Sorina makes no move to cover herself, occasionally glancing at the door to make sure she is still alone.

6:04 pm [Dylan: I am very disappointed, Sorina. I will have to punish you later. Get dressed and go back to work.]

She stares at the message, contemplating a response, but she sets it down on the albums with a sigh, bending down to pull up her pants. She has just finished putting herself to rights and walked back behind the counter when the door swings open, a handsome blonde man entering.

"Hey," she greets, taking a sip of her water bottle. Her hand smells like her pussy, and she hasn't had a chance to wash it yet. She will after the customer leaves.

He nods at her, a soft smile crossing his lips, and Sorina wonders what it would be like to kiss those lips. He seems vaguely familiar, but she can't place him. *Maybe he's come into the store before?*

She studies him as he walks down the opposite aisle, deft fingers flipping through the Ds. He reminds her of a hipster without the hat—plaid button-down shirt, dark jeans, shoulder-length hair, and a scruffy goatee that she wants to touch. She lets him skim for a while, watching the way he holds his body, the way he moves his hands, deciding that she wants to know what sounds he makes when he comes. *If only he'd come in a few minutes earlier, he'd have gotten quite a show...*

She glances at her phone, knowing she is supposed to text Dylan for permission any time she wants to fuck someone. She's allowed, of course. He wouldn't say no. But she's already disobeyed him by coming too soon, and if she asks now, he may deny her as punishment.

Sorina likes being punished—but she also likes coming on a hard cock—and right now, she wants this stranger in the store. She leans forward on the counter, propping her book up before her, knowing that if he glances over, he will see the outline of her ass in her jeans. A quick glance shows that he has been watching her, a little look here and there as he works his way through the three rows of Ds. When he begins skimming through the Es, she speaks.

"Help you find anything?" Her voice is low, sultry, and she gives him direct eye contact, loving how he meets her gaze. She narrows her eyes at him. "Let me guess: Depeche Mode?"

His smile reaches his eyes, and he tilts his head. "That obvious, huh?"

She shrugs. "I've worked here a while. We don't have anything from them in stock, but I can order it if you want." She pauses, then adds, "Looking for anything else?"

"How about the Bloodhound Gang?" he asks, a wicked smile teasing his lips.

"You looking for a little 'Bad Touch'?" she teases, hoping he follows her thoughts. The song is older, but his eyes light up in recognition.

He abandons the records, making his way around the aisle to stand in front of her. "That depends," he says, raising an eyebrow. "You up for some Discovery Channel?"

Sorina grins, putting her book down on the counter. "I don't know," she says, coming out from behind the counter, walking over to the Bs. The stranger follows her, and when she pauses, fingers flipping through the albums to reach the Bloodhound Gang, he steps up close behind her, body pressing against hers, soft breath on her neck. Sorina pushes back into him, her ass gently wiggling against his cock, pleased when she feels a sudden hardening press against her.

"Will we do it doggie style so we can both watch X-Files?" she sings, following the rhythm as she leans back into him, turning her face so his mouth finds hers, his lips soft. His hand grabs her hip and tugs her back against him even tighter, the other tangling in her hair. She moans at the pressure on her scalp, loving the way he moves her head around without asking.

The hand on her hip crawls up to cup her breast, and Sorina returns the favor, her hand snaking behind her to cup his cock through the jeans. He makes a muffled sound against her mouth, his tongue forcing its way deeper, and his hand slides down her body and into her jeans, bypassing her panties to press hard against her clit. Sorina almost comes right there at the stranger's touch, but then she remembers where they are. It's not like she hasn't fucked anyone at work before, but she's usually more careful. Then again, she's not always as worked up as she is right now, the fingering episode leaving her hungry for more action. Opening her eyes, she glances at the street. People hurry by outside, shadowy outlines in the late afternoon light, but no one enters.

The stranger's hand in her pants begins to move, fingers sliding back and forth across her clit, and she shudders, sensation swallowing her for a moment. She moans into his mouth, on the edge of orgasm again. She needs him inside of her.

Now.

He breaks the kiss to whisper against her lips, "Where?"

Sorina considers the end of the aisle again, but she doesn't want to risk leaning against the records and knocking anything over. He's taller than she is, so standing is definitely a possibility, but she's also wearing jeans, so even pulling them down will limit her range of motion. She doesn't want to risk taking them off completely, not while they are in the store.

Why didn't I wear a dress? The thought is fleeting—dresses at work are impractical given the amount of time she spends crawling around on the floor, though different clothing would make encounters like this one much easier.

She contemplates locking the door for a few minutes but decides against it. Another little rebellion, like not texting Dylan about her new friend. He's going to punish her so hard for this later tonight.

She can't wait.

"Behind the counter," she says after a moment, and he nods, stepping away from the rack of records, turning her body in front of his, and marching her around the counter. He leans her forward, her hands pressing against the glass top, then drags her jeans over her hips. She looks over her shoulder at him, watching his face as he appreciates the pink panties, then he smacks her ass, and she jolts forward, the shock blossoming into waves of pleasure.

"Oh yeah," she mumbles. "Like that!"

He grins, one hand working at the button of his jeans as the other winds up for another smack. She grunts at the impact, that warm flush vibrating though her, and she reaches around to help, pulling down his zipper and shorts in one quick tug, revealing a sizable hard cock. "Inside me," she demands. "Now."

"Yes, ma'am," he replies, then pushes her panties aside, sheathing himself in one hard stroke. Sorina cries out, both hands pressed flat against the counter to brace herself, but then he grabs one hand and tugs it behind her back, pressing it hard against her hip as he rocks into her again.

"God yes!" she cries as he thrusts again, but when she tries to push back against him, setting the rhythm hard and fast, he grabs her other hand and presses both against her back. Her breasts press hard into the countertop, the cool glass sliding against her rucked-up shirt. "More," she moans, loving the restraints while also wanting to move her body against his. The denied desire only drives her need for more— of everything. "More!" she demands.

The stranger moves behind her, three quick hard strokes pumping in and out. "More what?" he croons.

"More of that cock!" she demands, struggling to push back into him without her arms.

"Such a demanding girl," the stranger grunts, pounding into her with more force. He swats her ass again with his free hand, then digs his fingers into her hip and yanks her back to him. Sorina hopes she will have bruises tomorrow, a record of this chance encounter imprinted on her body. The idea is enough to send her shooting over the edge, and she shudders against him, squeezing tight as she comes. "Fuck yes," he groans, fucking her harder and faster. "Come on my cock again!" he demands, setting a brutal pace. Sorina squeals, the sound erupting out of her as she gets exactly what she wanted earlier when she fingered herself in the aisle. She looks up, watching the people on the street, wondering if her cries carry through the door. No one seems to notice, and she giggles at the naughtiness of it all—the public sex with a complete stranger...without texting Dylan first.

He's going to punish me so hard! The thought drives her over the cliff again, and she shudders against the stranger's cock, feeling him deep inside of her as he pumps harder. "Yes!" she cries. "Oh god yes!" The stranger releases her hip, grabbing her long ponytail of hair instead, twisting her head back as he yanks on it, pulling him into him with each thrust. "Yes fuck yes!" she yells again, not caring who hears her. The stranger pumps harder, hips shivering as he comes, his body leaning over on top of hers, both of them gasping for breath on top of the counter.

Oh yeah, Sorina thinks. *Tonight is going to be awesome.*

Chapter Three

At 9:58 that night, Sorina stands in her living room, proud of herself for being ready not only on time—but actually early. She still wears the pink bra and panties, but she traded her work jeans and t-shirt for a pink dress. The thigh high stockings were a last-minute addition, something to distract Dylan from the day's indiscretions, and she knows he will approve.

I hope he lets me go in the cage tonight.

They've been going to the sex club for months now, and while they have participated in several satisfying scenes, what Sorina really craves is time locked in the small cage, handcuffed and blindfolded while anyone can do anything to her. The blindfold makes it easy to give up control. If she can't see what's happening around her, she can't be paralyzed by indecision. She can let the moment swallow her, giving in to pure sensation, reveling in the ecstasy her body can provide.

At 10pm exactly, her front door opens. She turns to see Dylan striding inside, and something inside leaps at the sight of him, those long limbs, strong body, dark hair that catches the light just so. She had expected a text telling her to come downstairs and get in the car. Seeing him in her apartment means that her punishment will come sooner rather than later.

"Sorina," he says, and his voice makes her shiver. She loves hearing her name in his mouth. "You look perfect."

She dips her head, nodding in appreciation. "Thank you, Master."

He crosses the room, taking her in his arms and kissing her softly, gently. Sorina shivers, losing herself in his touch, knowing that while her master can be tender, he can also be wicked, and moments like these only enhance her excitement at what's coming. Breaking the kiss, he looks tenderly into her eyes. "Did you misbehave today, Sorina?" he whispers.

A chill runs through her. *Does he know about Tobin?* She'd learned her mystery lover's name before he left that evening. They'd exchanged numbers and made loose plans to meet again— preferably somewhere with a bed, he'd said. Dylan's face gives nothing away, and perhaps he is only referring to her minor indiscretion of coming without permission.

Well, minor in comparison to fucking someone without permission, of course. It's not cheating, not like that—she and Dylan are free to have sex with whomever they want whenever the occasion presents itself—but he ordered her to always ask first. This was partly another way of controlling her, freeing her from decision-making, but it was also about her safety. Sorina has fucked strangers in dangerous situations, only realizing afterward how easily the scene could have turned against her. Dylan promised to keep her safe—and texting is just another way of watching over her.

A tiny sliver of guilt works its way into her heart. *He's only trying to take care of me. I should let him.*

"I did," she replies, voice neutral as she looks away.

There is a long pause, but Sorina doesn't dare meet his gaze, knowing that he will ask her what she did. She won't lie to him, but if she can avoid mentioning Tobin until after she gets to spend time in the cage, she will. Finally, Sorina's nerve breaks, and she looks up at him. He raises an eyebrow, clearly deciding something, then he tuts his tongue. "So you did. And what do you think I should do about that?"

Sorina bites her lip, wondering what delightful punishment he has thought of. "I think you should punish me," she says quietly.

"Oh yes, and I will," he promises. "But how?"

This is new territory and something in Sorina's chest tightens at the question. The whole point of this relationship is that he relieves her of the burden of making choices. Having her choose her punishment breaks the rules in a terrible way. He must see the panic on her face because he speaks again.

"Don't you worry," he tells her. "I have something special worked out for tonight." He reaches down to put a hand inside one of his pockets, pulling out what look like thick rubber bands. "But first, let's get this settled." He kneels before her, a tap on the back of one leg the sign that she should put her heeled foot on his thigh. She watches as he slides her foot through one of the rubber bands, then proceeds to roll it up her leg to rest against her thigh, just at the top of her stockings. At her confused expression, he reaches between the band and her skin with one finger, a quick flick, and the band snaps back against her thigh. A sharp twang of pain lashes through her, and she jerks back, only Dylan's hands on her legs keeping her steady. She's never thought of rubber bands as a punishment before. She switches legs, allowing him to work the other band up her leg, settling it in place next to the other one. The top of her stocking offers some relief from the pinch and sting as he snaps it, but not a lot. She will have welts very soon.

Sorina expects him to put her foot back on the floor and stand, but instead, he glides his hands up her legs, taking a moment to snap both bands as he passes them, curling his hands around her ass beneath the dress. She lets herself lean into him, and he ducks his head beneath the skirt of her dress, breath hot against her skin. One hand traces the curve of her hip, and then he is sliding her panties down, just a little, enough to give him free access to her clit. His tongue is warm heaven as he licks her, and she sinks even more into him, but then a snap of the rubber band brings her out of the moment—and quickly into another kind of headspace.

"What did I say, Sorina?" he whispers, breath hot against her sensitive skin. "Remind me of what you were supposed to do."

Sorina shudders against him as he licks her again, fingers sliding against her skin in the way he knows she loves. "I...I was supposed to wait," she manages.

"You weren't a very good girl, Sorina," he tells, alternating a sweet lick with another snap, the pleasure and pain a delicious contrast. "You were a greedy girl. Are you a greedy girl?"

"I'm sorry, Master," she breathes, reaching below her dress to tangle her hands in his hair.

He looks up at her, eyes disappointed. "Where is my obedient Sorina?" he asks.

"I'm here, Master," she assures him. "I will obey you." She is rewarded by a long series of perfect pressure on her clit matched by sweet sliding fingers inside of her. "Oh, please..." she moans, close to the edge.

"Please what?" he encourages, returning to that sweet rhythm.

"Please let me come, Master!"

He rewards her words with a savage snap of both bands, and the heat in her belly explodes. She shudders against him, body reeling with release. "Thank you!" she gushes, hands pressing him hard against her. "Thank you!"

After sliding her panties back up to her hips, he leans back to look up at her, a lazy grin on his face. "I love watching you come," he says. "I can't wait to see you tonight."

Sorina bites her lip. "Is... tonight the night?" she whispers.

Dylan nods, then stands, taking both of her hands. "Let's go," he says.

Chapter Four

*D*ylan blindfolds her before they go inside the club, so Sorina has no real sense of the space around her. She's been inside before, though, so she remembers that the cage is near the entrance, situated so everyone walking inside can see the person inside. It's a small cage, maybe three feet across, with thin bars made for arms and legs to fit through easily—the better to tease the person inside. The cage is tall, and the cross bar across the top, intended to clip to cuffs or chains, can be moved up and down so the person can stand or sit inside.

He helps her inside. Sorina can hear the soft mumble of people talking, and Dylan greets several others as they head into the big room. She can feel the eyes on her, but she can't see anything but the velvety blackness in front of her, and the feeling is sublime. She allows herself to be led around, Dylan's strong hands on her hips and the small of her back as they move.

"Wait here," he orders, and Sorina obeys, standing as he instructed, her hands hanging loose at her sides. She can hear shuffling, movement, and she senses bodies nearby, but no one touches her. After a long moment, Dylan speaks again, his voice close to her ear. "Lift your arms," he tells her. Sorina obeys, and he lifts the dress over her head, the silky material sliding off her arms, her hair slipping down to touch her bare back. She wonders if she should pull her hair back, but then Dylan is touching her wrists, buckling the leather cuffs into place. He tugs her forward, and she steps over a small threshold, the ground beneath her high heels metal but with slight bumps all over.

Sorina imagines the diamond plate she's seen in factory floors, meant to allow people to keep their grip on the otherwise smooth surface. Her cuffed hand is raised above her head, and she hears the snick of the other end clicking into place. Another cuff touches her other hand, the velvet interior soft against her skin, and it too is raised above her head. Her hands have enough space to move side to side, though no more than the length of the cuff allows. Dylan moves away from her, and she hears the sound of a door swinging shut, the metal clang followed by sounds of locks sliding into place.

She examines her new space, pushing her arms out to test her range of motion. She's definitely cuffed to a point above her, probably in the center of the cage, but she can pull down far enough to bend her elbows, though she brushes against the cool metal bars of the cage if she does. Her legs are free, and she pushes her foot out slowly, heels dragging along the metal floor with a low scuffing noise, and she finds the edge of the cage. Her foot can fit between the bars, but only up to her shin, at which point the bars are too close together to move any more.

Without her sight, she focuses on her other senses—the low music in the background, something wordless with a slow sultry beat making her want to sway her hips if she listens to it too long. She can smell leather and the quiet bite of clean metal, her own deodorant and musky perfume wafting as her skin heats.

I wonder who is watching me right now. If anyone. I could be alone in this room and I wouldn't know.

But she knows that she isn't alone. She can hear the quiet voices around her, the low thud of someone being paddled, the soft moan of satisfaction. It's still early in the night, but she knows that soon those moans will get louder, more pervasive as the patrons loosen up and really unwind. This a private club: no phones, no evidence, and no rules beyond consent.

Sorina wonders if a stranger will fuck her tonight, if it's possible through the bars.

Tobin's face drifts through her mind, and she hopes she will see him again. He was delightful. The thought makes her wonder about Dylan—*does he know?* The rubber bands on her legs are certainly punishment, but they are for coming too soon. If he wanted to really punish her, he wouldn't let her in the cage with the blindfold on. He knows that's what she really craves—the anonymity of being captive and at everyone's mercy while unable to see who is touching her.

A hand traces along her thigh, and Sorina stiffens, not expecting the touch. The touch becomes a hand, the palm cupping her right thigh, and then someone snaps the rubber band around her other thigh, and she shudders. The hand moves up her thigh, over the line of her panties and pauses again on the soft skin of her stomach. Another finger glides along her shoulder, and Sorina wonders if they belong to the same person.

Maybe it's Dylan. Maybe not. Dylan likes to watch, will probably spend the whole night just watching other people touch her—only having his way with her at the very end, so he is the last one to claim her. The hand on her belly slides up to cup a breast, and Sorina bites her lip, hoping it will move to squeeze her nipple. A sudden snap of the rubber band shocks her, and she jerks away, moving back, and the hand cupping her breast twists to reach inside, pinching her nipple just as another hand touches her chin, running along her jawline, before slipping a finger inside her mouth. She sucks it in, trying to identify what she can. Probably a man, by the tough feel of the skin around the nail. It tastes faintly of soap, but not in a bad way, and she rotates her tongue around it, mimicking the motion she uses for a dick. There is a gasp nearby, someone enjoying himself, and another hand touches her lower leg, sliding up her calf as the hand in her bra continues to massage her nipple.

Definitely different people, she thinks, losing herself to sensation.

The first few touches are sweet, exploratory, but then one hand settles on her side and wiggles as if to tickle her. Sorina jerks back with a hiss, nearly biting the finger in her mouth, and a voice says, "Oh, yes. Tickle her." Sorina bites her lip in preparation. She doesn't enjoy tickling, hates the way her body reacts without her control, but here, trapped in the cage, blindfolded, handcuffed, and at a stranger's mercy, she gives herself over the feeling, giggling madly as the hand continues its relentless movement, hating the sensation even as she loves the release it offers. She is keenly aware of her body as a body, her sensitive skin over her bones teased as those questing fingers continue to explore every inch of her, seeking an even more ticklish spot. Fingers torment her armpits while others tickle her sides.

She still wears her heels, her bare feet protected from tickle torture. A hand wraps around her ankle, clearly intending to remove her shoe, but Dylan's quiet command stops the movement. His face must say something, because there are no more words, but the tickling focuses on the exposed parts of her body instead, and no one tries to take off her shoes. It's a tiny relief, a small part of herself that remains her own, safe from the abuse, though the rest of her enjoys the release of giving into the indignities of her skin, the snorting shrieks that escape her lips as she tries to twist away, only to find more tickling hands behind her.

Slowly, the tickles slow down, morphing into something more fluid, the touches on her skin sensual rather than teasing, and Sorina's skin sparks in response. She leans into the touches, body conflicted about which direction she wants to move. The hand on her stomach trails down to dip inside her panties while the hand on her shoulder dips down to pinch her nipple. Another hand snaps the band on her thigh, while yet another squeezes her ass. Sorina leans back, her body pressing into the cold bars behind her, and someone kisses a line up her neck, sliding her hair over her shoulders to trail over her breasts. Another hand finds its way into her panties from behind, fingers dipping between her cheeks to circle her asshole. She sighs, pressing back into the touch, and then her arms are being lowered, the hands encouraging her to her knees. Sorina obeys, hands still held above her head, but now with plenty of room for her to kneel. The metal floor bites into her skin, and she bites her lip, the dull ache welcome against the sharp snap along her thighs as someone snaps the band again. She flattens her feet in the heels, the top of her foot resting on the floor and reminds herself to stay upright so she doesn't spike herself accidentally. Her thighs will already be a mess tomorrow— she doesn't want to add a scrape from heels to the party.

That's not the kind of pain she wants anyway.

Hands gently touch her face, more fingers pressing against her lips, seeking entrance, and then she is sucking on them. These are smaller fingers, delicate, and the smooth nails suggest polish or gel—maybe a woman's hands? The fingers coax her forward, mouth following along, and then something else is before her lips. She recognizes the cock immediately, enjoys how the hand on her face seems to guide the cock into her mouth. She leans forward eagerly, circling the tip with her tongue and wrapping her lips around it, sucking a little to pull it closer. It doesn't move, the owner probably pressed up against the bars, so she leans forward more, her arms tugging on the cuffs as she reaches the edge of her reach. More hands stroke her head, tugging her hair out of the way as she sucks more of the cock in her mouth. She wonders whose cock it is, whether it's another stranger or someone she knows, and she listens hard, ears straining for the sounds of heavy breathing she knows she must be eliciting from her partner.

Instead, she gasps as two hands pull her back by her hips, her butt pressed up against the bars as a hand moves her panties aside and runs along her slit. Another hand works around her front, rubbing her clit in rhythmic circles while the other hand continues to run up and down her opening. She groans, sucking harder on the cock in her mouth, and pushes back into the hands. Another hand reaches inside her bra and pinches her nipple while yet another snaps the band on her thigh. She squeals, the sensations flooding her, the warm heat in her belly pooling and rising through her center. The pressure on her clit continues, and soon she is sliding over the edge, her body tightening with release. Fingers weave their way through her hair, seemingly connected to the cock in her mouth, and Sorina sucks harder, tugging the stranger over the edge with her. Cum fills her mouth, and she swallows reflexively. The cock hovers for a moment, the hands still tight on her head, but then they release, and the cock slips out of her mouth.

She pauses for a moment, catching her breath, but the hands return to her panties, this time sliding them down over her ass to hover around her thighs. The fingers become more insistent, sliding inside of her while another hand restarts those small circles on her clit. She moans, licking her lips, and then another cock is pressing against her cheek, a trail of cum leaving wetness across her skin before the head finds her mouth.

At the same time, the fingers inside of her move aside, migrating to circle her asshole instead as a hard cock presses against her opening. Sorina squeals with glee, pressing her ass hard against the bars, giving the cock more access to her pussy, and the head slips between her lips, just pressing gently inside of her opening. The cock in her mouth surges forward at the same time, and two new hands cup her breasts, pulling them free of the bra and squeezing her nipples in tandem with the cock pulsing in her mouth and the other teasing her opening.

Oh fuck yes!

She presses back again, wanting to encourage the cock behind her, but the cage prevents her from claiming him. Her hands flail against the cuffs with a metal clang as she tries to move her body and control the motion, demanding more.

"Oh no, Sorina," Dylan's voice coos nearby. "You don't get to set the rules here. You just get to experience it. Let it happen."

Sorina's body relaxes instantly, sagging into the hands around her, the soft feel of manicured nails running through her hair while she sucks the cock in her mouth slowly, enjoying the feel of the soft warm skin against her tongue. The cock barely in her pussy slides forward slowly, a tiny fraction at a time, and the fingers massaging her asshole slide inside just a little bit. The hand on her clit continues to rub in steady circles, and Sorina feels another orgasm building inside.

She can hear heavy breathing around her, and the telltale slap of hands on cocks, and she wonders who is jerking off nearby. An image forms in her mind, a circle of men standing all around the cage, all with their dicks in hand, jerking off as they watch the stranger fuck her from behind while she sucks the other man's cock. The idea is enough to make her nipples harden again, her core tightening, and she shudders again, body expanding in pleasure.

The cock inside her begins to move in earnest, filling her pussy more with each stroke. The cock in her mouth twitches, and Sorina knows he is close. She uses her teeth a little, nibbling along the head just a touch, and the cock twitches even more. If she didn't have a cock in her mouth, Sorina would smile.

The hands squeeze her nipples again, and hands grip her hips, holding her immobile against the cage as the cock plows in and out. Her knees ache, and then someone snaps the bands on her thighs, and the pain streaks through her like a brand, and she comes harder, body jerking as the waves of pleasure wash her away. The cock in her mouth explodes, shooting warm cum down her throat, and the cock in her pussy pumps hard two, three more times before filling her with warmth, the hands gripping her hips hard. At the same moment, warm patches of heat strike her skin all over, the men around the cage coming in a round circle of release.

The cock in her mouth pulls away, and Sorina licks her lips, body singing in satisfaction. She is completely in the moment, completely content in herself.

Then Dylan enacts her punishment.

Hands tug the blindfold from her head. She is blinded for a moment, the dim lights of the club too bright for her sensitive eyes, but soon enough, the world swims back into focus. She stares through the bars of the cage to see Tobin standing in front of her, a perfect smile on his face. Dylan stands next to him, a hand on his shoulder.

Sorina glances madly around, panic swirling through her at the sight of so many people leaning against the cage, some with hands still reaching between the bars to touch her. Many of the men have their cocks out, and she glances behind her, wondering which of the three men standing back there was just fucking her. She vaguely recognizes some familiar faces, but no one she has played with before. Shame fills her, and even as it does, part of her rejoices at the sensation, the humiliation of being locked in this cage and covered with strangers' cum. She turns her head forward again, looking up into Dylan's face.

"Is there something you want to tell me, Sorina?" Dylan croons, kneeling down so his face is level with hers. "Something you'd like to confess?"

"I..." Sorina stalls, not sure what to say. Tobin stands there, perfectly comfortable, so clearly he's in on it. She wants to be annoyed with him, but she can't find the feeling. Instead, she wants him to fuck her again, this time with Dylan and everyone else watching. "I may have forgotten to text you, Master," she mumbles.

"What was that, Sorina?" he prompts, a hand stroking her cheek, scooping up a stray line of cum and sliding it into her mouth.

She swallows, then repeats herself in a louder voice. "Forgive me," she adds.

"And here I sent you a gift," Dylan says, shaking his head, "knowing how much you like to be fucked after fingering yourself. I knew you would want more, and Tobin here was quite eager to make your acquaintance, especially after what he saw last time we were here."

Sorina bites her lip. *So, that's why he was familiar*, she thinks.

"Tell me, Sorina, how was he?" Dylan purrs. "Did you enjoy my gift?"

"He was amazing," she says honestly. "So good."

Dylan nods approvingly. "I'm glad to hear it. Unfortunately, you're going to have to wait until you've been properly punished before you get to enjoy him again."

Chapter Five

*D*ylan approaches and unlatches the cage door. He reaches inside, carefully avoiding her body. When Dylan unhooks her cuffs from the bar overhead, he tugs gently, and she gets clumsily to her feet. She stumbles, and several people reach through the bars to steady her, their fingers an odd mixture of hot and cold, smooth and clammy, as they help her to her feet.

Pins and needles slowly work their way down her lower legs, the top of her feet burning as sensation pours back into her. She sways dangerously, and Dylan collects her in his arms, tugging her close before he swings her body up against his chest, lifting her out of the cage. She sags against him, hardly noticing when one high heel thumps to the metal floor of the cage. She snuggles absently into his chest, relishing the security of his closeness, knowing that her reprieve is only temporary, that she still needs to be properly punished.

The idea sparks something deep within, and she smiles, twisting her face away from his chest to take in the room around her. Dylan carries her away from the cage to a bench set beneath another length of chain suspended from the ceiling. Sorina notes the empty ring at the bottom, perfectly placed to cuff her to, keeping her arms above her head. Her shoulders already ache from being in that position, but she's excited to repeat the posture, especially being able to see her partners, knowing that without the cage between them, anyone will be able to touch her in any way they want.

A shiver runs through her, and Dylan looks down, nodding when he sees that she is recovered and ready for the next round. He gives her a soft, secret smile meant only for her, then sets her down on the bench, one leg on each side. His hands run down the length of her legs as he lets her go, but he snaps one of the rubber bands with a wink before lifting her arms above her head again and attaching the cuffs to the chain above. He steps back, allowing a woman and Tobin to take his place. The woman is lovely, a petite brunette with bouncy curls surrounding her face, and she bites her lip as she sits in front of Sorina.

"You are so sexy," she says quietly, reaching up to push Sorina's hair behind an ear. "May I kiss you?"

Sorina nods, leaning forward to meet her new friend's soft lips. The kiss is gentle, sweet, and another pair of hands begins to rub Sorina's shoulders from behind. She glances down, opening her eyes to study the fingers and recognizes Tobin's big hands. He rubs hard, easing the sore muscles of her shoulders before sliding over to work her neck, fingers running through her hair and along her scalp. The woman runs a hand up from Sorina's waist, brushing along the edge of her bra, and she looks down at it, a question in her eyes. Sorina nods, glad that Dylan chose a bra with removable straps so that when Tobin unclips the back, she can tug the straps free and pull the bra completely away, instead of it lingering around her arms and head somewhere above her. The woman bends her head down, taking Sorina's nipple into her mouth, and Sorina moans, the warm heat thrilling. She's had many men suck her nipples, but there is something different about a woman's mouth, the fullness of her lips, the gentle press of her tongue, that makes the heat pool in Sorina's belly.

Tobin's hands begin sliding down her back to rest on her hips, and she pushes back into him, trying to get a sense of where his body is without looking away from the woman nuzzling her nipples.

"Oh, honey," the woman says, "I think I need to taste you." Sorina grins, and Tobin's hands on her hips lift her up off the bench just enough to slide her panties down. The woman takes them from her side, lifting one of Sorina's legs back over the bench so her legs are on the same side of the bench as her panties slide off her ankles. The woman runs both hands back up Sorina's legs, pausing the snap one of the rubber bands with a wicked wink, before she tugs the leg back over to the other side again, spreading Sorina wide and pressing her back on the bench. Sorina's arms move forward as her body lays back, the slack in the cuffs enough to let her dangle at a 45-degree angle from the bench. The movement changes the strain on her arms, and she sighs, enjoying the pull forward and up rather just straight up.

Tobin is sitting behind her, and her back lands against his bare chest. He leans down to nuzzle her neck, then moves over to claim her mouth. At the same time, the woman pushes forward, her warm breath teasing Sorina's clit, and she moans into Tobin's mouth. The woman has small deft fingers that she slides just inside, pressing up in a rhythm that matches her tongue on Sorina's clit. Pleasure explodes through Sorina, and her body tightens, hands jerking against the cuffs as she longs to run her fingers through the woman's hair, to hold her head, guiding this way and that. Not that the stranger needs much guidance, her skilled fingers and tongue bringing Sorina right to the edge and over in a matter of moments.

She screams into Tobin's mouth. The woman only pauses a moment, then continues her motion. A soft gasp against her skin makes Sorina open her eyes and look down. She grins, looking up to meet the man's eyes who has positioned himself behind her new friend, hard cock pressing against her. The woman looks over her shoulder, bobs her head in assent, then returns to her work between Sorina's thighs. Her friend's hands and mouth continue to work beautifully, the rhythm now enhanced by the slow steady pulse of the man fucking her with long thrusts. He watches Sorina as he fucks the woman, biting his lip. He grips her hips, fucking her harder for a moment, then pauses to pull back and slap her ass. The woman bucks in pleasure, her mouth sucking hard on Sorina's clit, and she smiles at the stranger, eyefucking him while Tobin's hands slide down to pinch her nipples. Her body tightens, on the brink of release, and then she is coming hard.

The woman between her legs looks up, satisfaction on her face as she pushes back against the man fucking her and smiles. "I think I need you to sit on my face," she suggests, spinning around to put her back on the bench, looking up at Sorina expectantly. The man between her legs kneels so he can continue to fuck her, and Tobin helps Sorina stand up with one leg on either side of the bench. He tugs on the chain overhead, and it clicks up a few inches, allowing Sorina to stand with her arms overhead again. She hovers over the woman's face, her lipstick smudged around her full lips, shiny with Sorina's juices, and her new friend reaches out to wrap her arms around Sorina's hips, finding the same sweet spot with her tongue.

Sorina's head falls back in pleasure, and she closes her eyes for a moment, lost in sensation. She feels movement in front of her, and when she opens her eyes, Tobin is standing on the bench before her, pants unbuttoned and his cock just above the level of her mouth. She reaches for him, and the woman tightens her grip on her hips, tugging her down again. Sorina strains more, barely managing to lick the tip of Tobin's cock, her need for more growing with each determined suck between her legs. Tobin smiles above her where he holds the chain with one hand to keep himself steady. He bends his knees a little, allowing Sorina to suck his cock in her mouth in one desperate move, and she teases him with her tongue.

The moment is perfect: the mouth between her legs, the cock in her mouth, the eyes of the people watching their show, the sounds of fucking so close and yet not her own.

Not yet.

She is about to come again, then Tobin stands up straight, his cock slipping out of her mouth. She frowns, making a disappointed noise at his exit, but then his hands are in her hair again, wrapping it around his hand and pressing hard. A stranger snaps the band around her thigh and she jerks, her hair pulling tight against her scalp, and then she is coming again, savagely riding the woman's face. Tobin seems to sense her need because he tugs on the chain, letting her down again, but instead of allowing her to settle on the bench when the woman scoots down and sits up, her attention focused on the man fucking her now, Tobin sits beneath her, settling her on his lap, his hard cock pressed against her entrance.

"You want me down in your South Seas?" he quotes the Bloodhound Gang again, and Sorina laughs, pushing forward and onto him in one thrust. His hands curve around her hips and ass as he moves in her, setting a devastating rhythm. Sorina surrenders to him, surprised to find herself satisfied with just one partner, but relieved that she can focus on singular sensations at last—the touch of her hands on her ass, the press of his mouth against hers, the fullness of his cock sliding in and out of her pussy. The orgasm builds slowly despite the frenetic pace, and Tobin's hand returns to her hair, tugging her hair back. The glow in her belly ignites again.

"Look at me," he demands. "I want to watch you come on my cock, beauty."

Sorina obeys, coming hard and fighting to keep her eyes open to stare at him. He smiles at her, pleased, and when his eyes close for a moment, preparing for his own pleasure, Sorina glances over his shoulder to where

Dylan stands a few feet away, face hungry as he watches her. She smiles at her master, pleased despite the punishment, knowing that while she loves the feeling of invisibility behind the blindfold, there is another part of her that thrives on exhibitions like this, and he has punished her with a reminder of that joy.

"Come for me," he mouths at her, and her body obeys, tightening around Tobin's cock as he grunts, coming for her, and they both slide over the edge together.

Oh yes, Sorina thinks, *punishment indeed.*

Chapter Six

*L*ater, Tobin carries her into her apartment, setting her gently on the bed. He takes off her shoes, even the one reclaimed from the cage floor as they left the club. As he slides her stockings down, his touch is gentle, practical, but not sexual. Sorina is sensually exhausted, her body on the edge of endurance, wrung out from so many orgasms and the overload of touch and satisfaction. His fingers are extremely gentle as he removes the rubber bands, careful not to let them touch or pull her skin on the way down, fingers stretched out around her legs in a protective embrace. Her thighs have concurrent rings of red around them, welts that will surely sting even more when he gets her in the shower.

She knows that's where this is heading. Dylan often bathes her after a long night like this, her normally severe master quiet and soothing as he cleans her and puts her to bed. She raises her arms automatically to let him tug the dress free, though the motion makes her back and shoulders ache. He removes her bra and panties before leading her into the bathroom. He turns the water on, then quickly undresses as they wait for the water to heat up.

She is not so far gone that she doesn't appreciate the lines of his body as he stands naked before her, but his cock is only slightly hard, knowing that what she needs right now isn't more fucking.

When the water is warm, he helps her inside the shower stall, letting her stand beneath the spray as he begins to lather soap in his hands. He begins with her feet, washing them and sliding up her legs. He does not soap her thighs near the red welts, knowing that the burn will be too intense, settling for a thorough soaping of her ass and pussy instead. Her belly is next, and he massages her breasts with soap before finishing with her armpits and arms.

He shampoos her hair next, fingers massaging her scalp, then unhooks the shower head and sprays the remaining soap from her body. When he is finished, he uses the conditioner, running his fingers through her hair and finger combing the worst tangles, using the slippery cream to detangle as much as possible. He lets the conditioner sit for a moment, rubbing her shoulders and neck with his strong fingers.

When she sighs, leaning back against him, he rinses her a final time, careful to remove all of the soap and conditioner before turning off the water and wrapping her in a large towel. He slings a towel around his hips quickly, just to catch the dripping, then resumes his care, patting her dry with the towel and leading her back to the bed. He works on her hair, brushing it out with slow steady strokes, then stands up to pull out a nightshirt from her dresser. He returns to the bathroom with her towel to hang it up and comes back to kneel before the bed, a tube of first aid cream in one hand as he rubs the soothing cream over the welts on her legs. She will have bruises, but those don't require care.

He tugs the long shirt over her head, lifting her hair over the neck, then pulls the blankets down, settling her against the pillow and tucking the blanket over her. She can hear him moving around her apartment after that, but Sorina is barely aware of it. She does rouse when he lifts a straw to her lips, a soft command to drink making her turn her head enough to sip the water he has provided. He sets the water bottle on the nightstand, then continues moving around her apartment some more.

The next time Sorina opens her eyes, the lights are off, and he is getting into bed beside her, tucking her into his chest the way she likes. She snuggles into him, her master, safe and content in his arms.

In the middle of the night, he wakes her with soft kisses, making love to her with a gentleness that breaks the remains of her walls. His cock is hard inside of her, but he moves slowly, an easy rhythm that she sinks into, her body building to a release that surprises her in its intensity. She didn't think she had any more orgasms in her tonight, but Dylan proves her wrong, his touch soft but insistent. Gentle he may be—denied he would not. She knows that watching her with others excites him, and sometimes their fucking is intense and passionate. Other times, especially after nights like this, he lifts her back into the world of sensation with inexorable patience, and her body sings in release. It's not the same as the strong orgasms she has with strangers; it's something more soulful, and it's the reason why Dylan is the one who takes her home.

Satisfied in another way, Sorina drifts back into sleep with Dylan still on top of her, his softening cock still inside of her. In the morning, she is awakened by a familiar voice in her ear.

"Wake up Sorina," her master whispers.

ALI WHIPPE

Ali Whippe is the pen name of a professor in the higher education system who delights in imagining naughty distractions while enduring endless mind-numbing committee meetings. She loves to push the boundaries of the ritten word and the imagination, knowing that life at work would be way more exciting if more people didn't wear panties.

Naked with New Jersey Devil

Laying with the Lady in Blue

Wanton Woman in White

Beating it with Bloody Mary

Beau and Professor Bestialora

The Goat's Gruff

Goldie and Her Three Beards

Pied Piper's Pipe

Princess Pea's Bed

Pinnochio and the Blow Up Doll

Jack's Beanstalk

LGBT Erotica

Grayson Ace

How I Got Here

First Year Out of the Closet

You're Only a Top?

You're Only a Bottom?

I Think I'm a Serial Swiper

Lookin in All the Wrong Places

Leo Sparx

Before Alexander

Claiming Alexander

Taming Alexander

Saving Alexander

Dominic Ashen

Steel & Thunder

Storms & Sacrifice

4HorsemenPublications.com